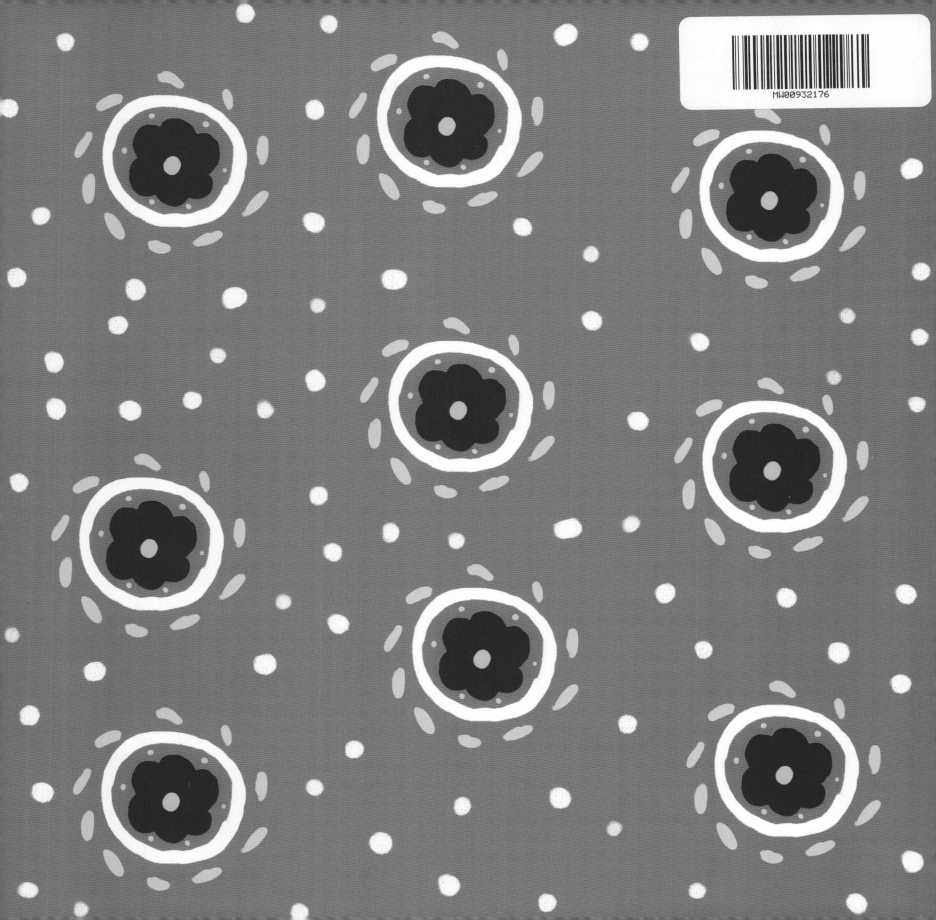

For Ireolúwa.
My eardrums still tingle from your
earth-shattering tantrums.

Thank you for the inspiration.

—A.O.

Copyright © 2023 by Àlàbá Ònájìn

All rights reserved. Published in the United States by Random House Studio,
an imprint of Random House Children's Books,
a division of Penguin Random House LLC, New York.

Random House Studio with colophon is a registered trademark of Penguin Random House LLC.

Visit us on the Web! rhcbooks.com

Educators and librarians, for a variety of teaching tools, visit us at RHTeachersLibrarians.com

Library of Congress Cataloging-in-Publication Data is available upon request.
ISBN 978-0-593-64407-2 (trade)
ISBN 978-0-593-64408-9 (lib. bdg.)
ISBN 978-0-593-64409-6 (ebook)

The artist used Procreate to create the illustrations for this book.
The text of this book is set in 23-point Golden Type ITC.
Interior design by Rachael Cole and Paula Baver

MANUFACTURED IN CHINA
10 9 8 7 6 5 4 3 2 1
First Edition

Waaa Waaa

GOES TÁWÁ

Àlàbá Ònájìn

RANDOM HOUSE STUDIO ⌂ NEW YORK

Mama is off to the market.
But Táwà wants to go with Mama.

"No, no, Táwà.

Stay and play with Grandma."

goes Táwà!

"Okay, Táwà. All right, Táwà. Let's go together," says Mama.

Táwà and Mama head
to the market.
Táwà wants a doll.

"No, no, Táwà. You have plenty of dolls," says Mama.

"Here, Táwà, take the doll,"
the toy seller says.
"Please stop crying!"

Little Olá wants to play with Táwà's new doll.

But Táwà does not want to share.

And

Waa

goes Táwà!

"No, no, no," says Mama.

Little Olá doesn't want to play with Táwà anymore.

Táwà and Mama walk into
the hairdresser's shop.

"Time for new braids, Táwà!" says Mama.

"That's it, Táwà. No braids today.

We're going right home."

Papa is back from work.

"No, Táwà. Not now. Papa is very tired," he says.

And goes Táwà.

It's bedtime.

Papa, Mama, and Grandma can rest now.

"Táwà, please! Please, please stop crying!"

"Shhhh. You're going to wake the whole neighborhood!"

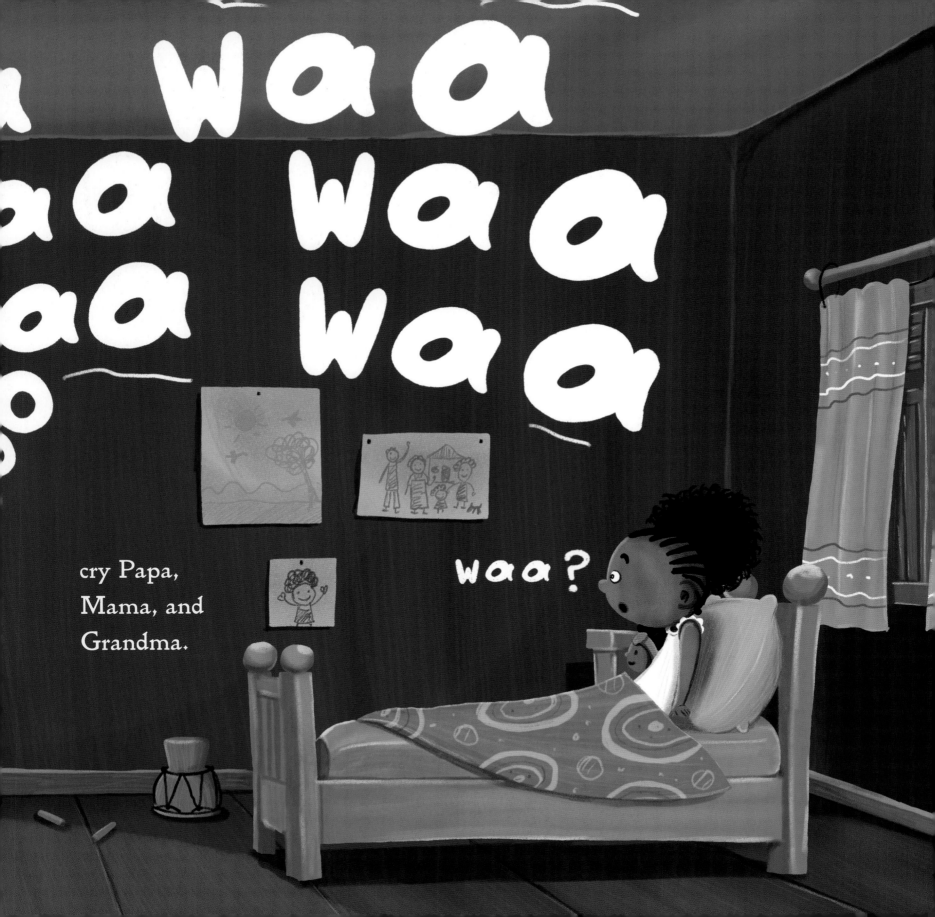

Waa Waa Waa
aa Waa Waa
aa Waa

waa?

cry Papa,
Mama, and
Grandma.

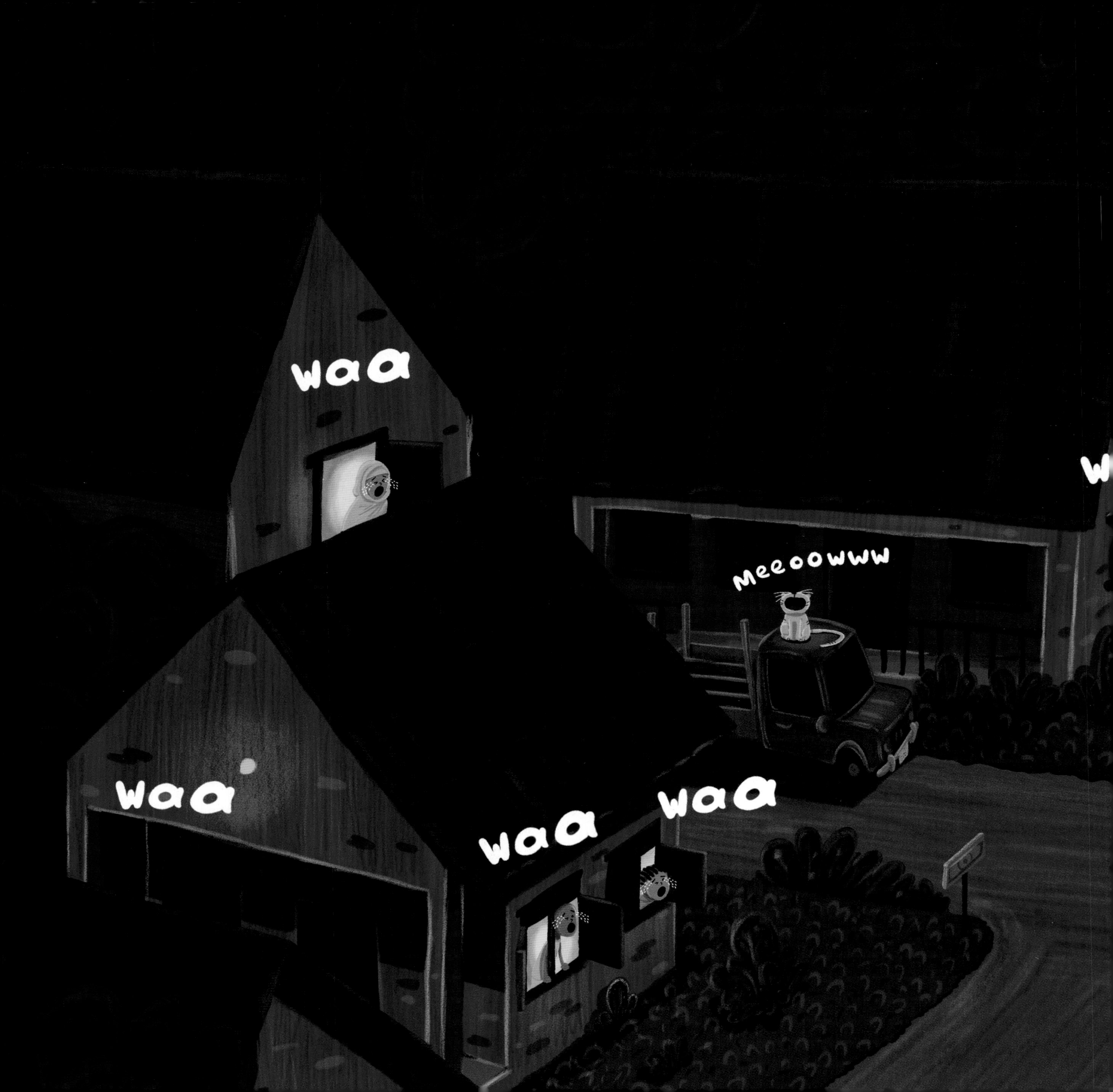
waa
Meeoowww
waa
waa
waa

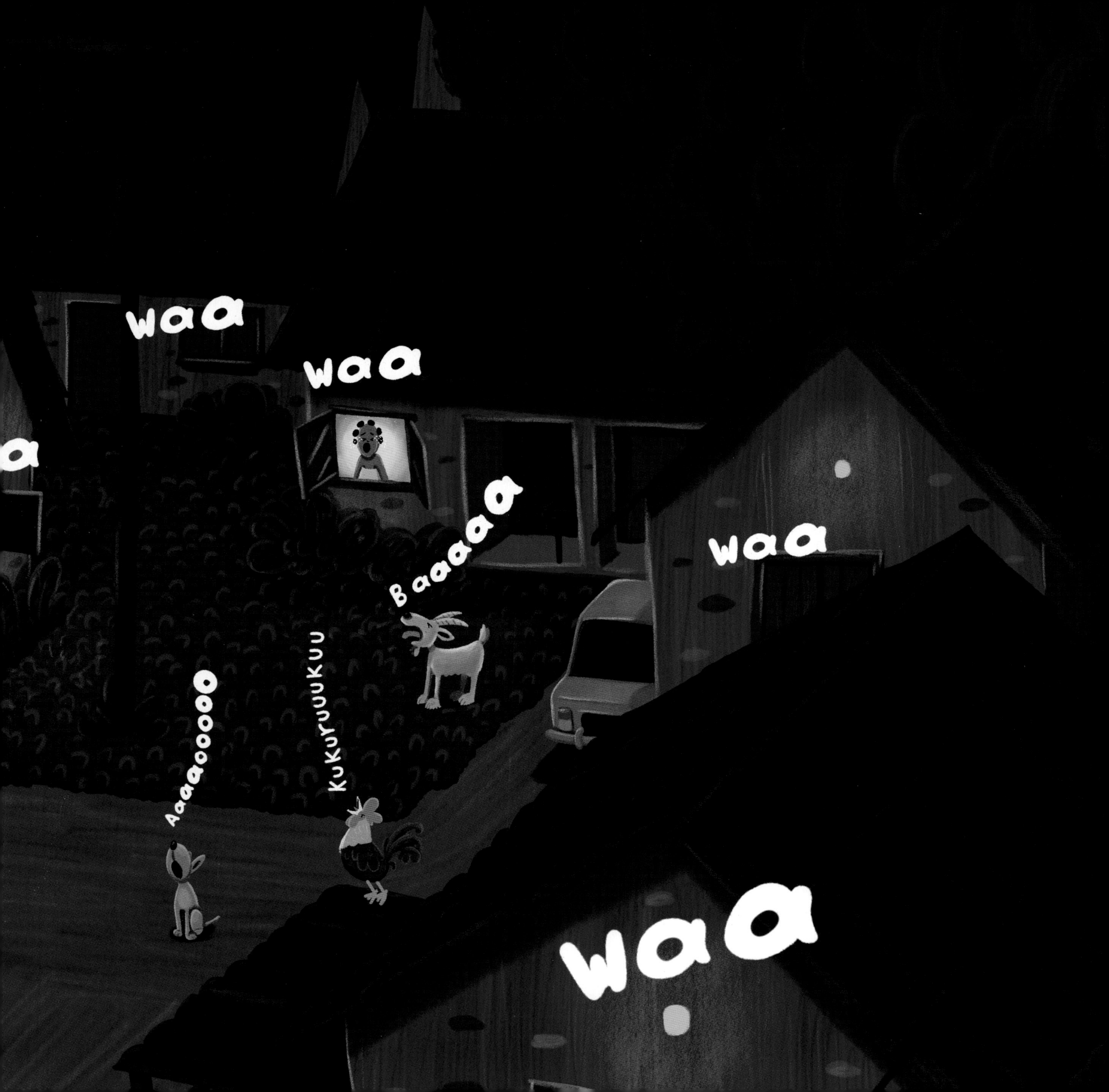
waa
waa
Baaaaa
waa
KuKuruuuuKuu
Aaaaooooo
waa

"Shhhhh! Don't be sad!" says Táwà.

"Night-night, sweet Táwà.

Sleep tight."

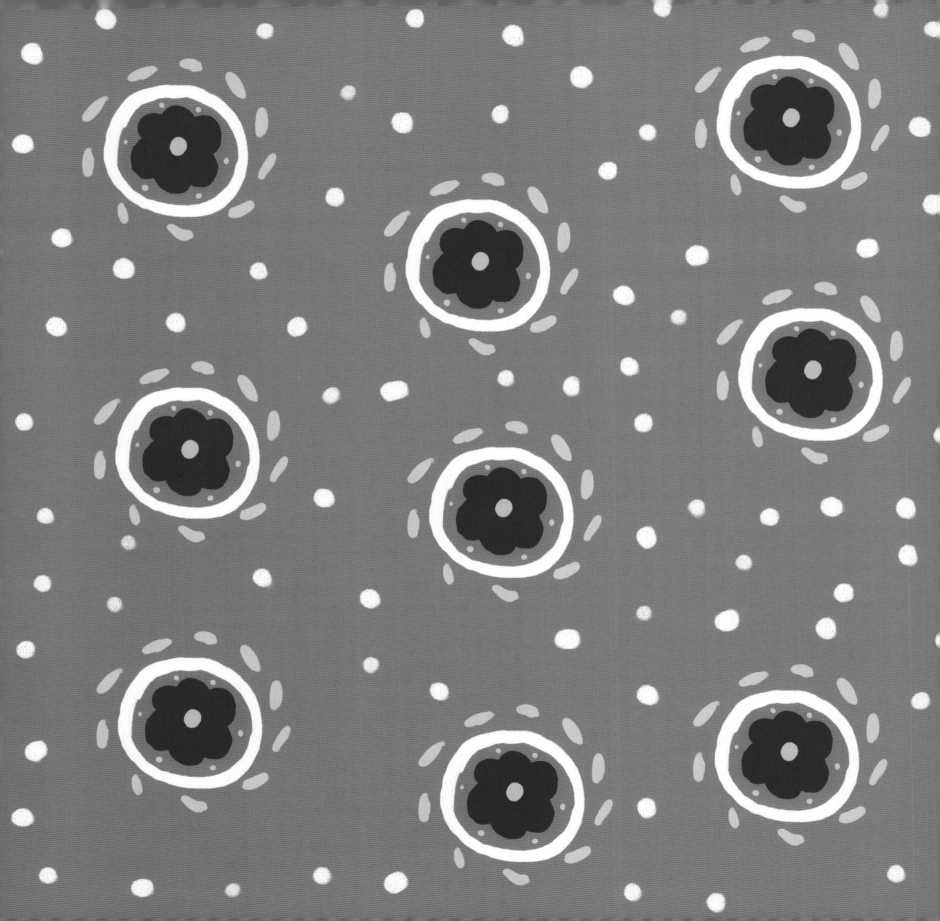